BOOKER
THE LIBRARY BAT
THE NEW GUARD

By **Jess M. Brallier** • Illustrated by **Jeff Harter**

PIXEL✚INK

*To librarians. For your bravery, for your care,
and for providing haven to writers and readers.* —J.B.

For Mom and Dad, who I may have driven a little batty at times as a kid. —J.H.

PIXEL✚INK

Text copyright © 2022 by Jess M. Brallier
Illustrations copyright © 2022 by Jeff Harter

Pixel+Ink is an imprint of TGM Development Corp.
www.pixelandinkbooks.com
Printed and bound in June 2022 at C&C Offset, Shenzhen, China.
Book design by Jay Colvin

Library of Congress Cataloging in Publication Data
Names: Brallier, Jess M., author. | Harter, Jeff, illustrator.
Title: The new guard / Jess Brallier ; illustrated by Jeff Harter.
Description: First edition. | New York : Pixel+Ink, [2022] | Series: Booker
the library bat ; 1 | Audience: Ages 4-7. | Audience: Grades K-1.
Summary: Booker the bat, new to his job as a security guard at the
Joanine Library, foils the attempted theft of pages from one of the
collection's rare books.
Identifiers: LCCN 2022005999 (print) | LCCN 2022006000 (ebook)
ISBN 9781645950462 (hardback) | ISBN 9781645951216 (ebook)
Subjects: CYAC: Bats—Fiction. | Libraries—Fiction. | LCGFT: Animal
fiction. | Picture books.
Classification: LCC PZ7.B73358 Ne 2022 (print) | LCC PZ7.B73358 (ebook)
DDC [E]—dc23
LC record available at https://lccn.loc.gov/2022005999
LC ebook record available at https://lccn.loc.gov/2022006000

Hardcover ISBN: 978-1-64595-046-2
E-book ISBN: 978-1-64595-121-6

First Edition

1 3 5 7 9 10 8 6 4 2

BATS AND BOOKS

At the Joanine Library in Coimbra, Portugal, bats have guarded books from book-eating bugs for over 200 years. The 12 or so bats sleep out of sight in the library during the day and then come out at night to hunt.

Each bat, in a single night, eats up to 500 of the bugs that buzz around the library's 200,000 leather-bound books. That's a lot of bug eating and a lot of bat pooping.

The bats' bodies are only 1½ to 2 inches long, but their wingspan can be nearly 10 inches. Bats emit sounds and listen for echoes to determine where things are. This is called "echolocation." It's the perfect skill for an animal who flies around in the dark.

What follows is the imagined story of one of those library bats.

The bat's hairy wings turn a book page.
His buggy eyes follow the words.
And his piggy nose wiggles.

Booker is the library's newest guard.

Booker always hoped to be a guard.
Even when he was tinier than he is now.
Work in a library? Yeah! I love books.

A guard's job is to eat bugs, before those
bugs eat books.

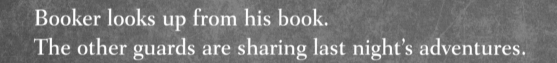

Booker looks up from his book.
The other guards are sharing last night's adventures.

This is Booker's first night on the job.
It feels like his first day at school.
Or like when his family moved to a new attic.
What if I don't fit in?

Booker watches Rocco.

Cool guard. Confident. Uses a bit of gel in his fur.

Rocco grins. "Last night, I goofed around and danced on a man's head."

Booker worries. *Will I have to scare people?*

Teddy likes to talk about eating.
"I had green bugs from near the lemon trees.
They really made me poop!"

Then Tess jumps in.
Head up high, legs wide, Tess spreads her wings. "I ate a moth this big!"
And then she burps.
All the bats laugh.
Will I be funny enough?

Rocco says, "Okay, that's enough. Let's get to work."
He turns to Booker. "Joining us?"

"Thanks, but since this is my first night, I should go explore the library."

Rocco grins. "Okay, kid."

The other guards go off to eat library bugs. After that, they'll leave the library for the night, to play and seek adventure.

Booker flies to his right.
He uses echolocation to find his way.

There! A light hangs from the ceiling. Booker just
misses it, then he senses bugs below! He dives. *Chomp!*
Booker licks his lips.
Not bad!

He goes through a door and
turns left down a hall.
More bugs. *Chomp!*

The other guards finished their rounds, so Booker's now alone in the dark library. He flies down a hall, then up a staircase. So many books! He turns and—

Hold on! What's that?

There's light coming from a room. It's the rare book room! Booker looks in.

A man with a flashlight rolls out from beneath a table. He must have hidden there before the library closed.

The man takes an old book from a shelf. The book's pages have beautiful paintings on them.

Then he pulls out a dagger.
Oh no!
Booker's heart jumps.
This can't be good!

The man sets the flashlight on the table, and starts
to cut pages from the book.

I know! People need light to see.
I read about that in a book. That's why he has the flashlight!

Booker spreads his wings.

Then dives at full speed and slams into the flashlight.

But his little body bounces off.

Ouch!

That didn't work.

Booker flies back up to
the ceiling to think. The
man cuts out another page.
*If only the other guards
were—*
    *Rocco! What would
Rocco do?*
    That's it!

Booker takes a deep breath. And zooms toward the man.
Boing! Booker lands on the man's head.
The man swats at Booker but misses.
Booker dances on the man's head just like Rocco did.
Then retreats to a shelf.

The man slips the dagger back into his pocket.

He looks up at Booker. For tonight, the little bat has stopped the thief.

"But I'll return. With a bat trap!"

The man throws a tarp over the table, and crawls back under.

Oh boy, oh boy. He'll slip out when the library opens in the morning. He'll get a bat trap. Then he'll get me. Then more books! What can I do? What can I do?

Hold on.

The other guards said, "Never dirty the floor!"

That's it! I'll poop right next to the table. That's going to upset the librarians. But when they clean the floor, they'll find that man under the table.

Booker goes to poop.

But uh-oh.

Nothing!
What would the other guards—

*That's it! What Teddy said earlier.
About the bugs at the lemon trees
making him have to poop!*

Booker quickly slips out of the library.
He flies over an old house where he once lived.
Over the school where he first read.
Past the bell tower where it's too noisy to hang out.
He's nearly to the lemon trees.

And look who's there! Tess, Rocco, and Teddy!

"Help! Help!" Booker yells. "A bad guy . . . with a dagger!"

Tess holds up her wings. "Take a breath, Booker. How can we help?"

"I need you to poop at the library."
Booker explains his plan.
Rocco smiles. "Very cool, Booker. Okay guys, eat up!"
Soon enough, their tummies are full of bugs.

They all fly to the library.
Booker shows them where the bad guy's hiding.
Tess aims for the floor next to it. *Blam!*
Then Teddy. *Blam!*
Then Rocco. *Blam, blam!*
Rocco high-wings Booker. "They'll see that mess for sure!"
Booker smiles. "We're making *good* trouble."

Booker and the other guards keep watch until morning, when the cleaners arrive with mops and buckets of soapy water.

The cleaners are angry about the mess. But then one pushes his mop under the table and the burglar is found.

Booker's plan worked!

That night, the guards gather to talk about their most recent adventures.

Teddy wants to tell Booker about the juicy-looking moths he saw.

And Tess wants to show Booker how she did a flip from the bell tower.

But Rocco quiets them.
He looks at Booker. "You go first, buddy."

Booker smiles. *They like me.*